For Ilse, Maya and Soon-Dae

Library of Congress Cataloging-in-Publication Data

Spetter, Jung-Hee, 1969-
    [Zon en zee. English]
    Lily and Trooper's summer / Jung-Hee Spetter. — 1st American ed.
        p.   cm.
    Summary: A little girl and her dog revel in the many joys of a
    summer day.
    ISBN 1-886910-37-5
[1. Summer—Fiction. 2. Dogs—Fiction.] I. Title.
PZ7.S7515Liu   1999
    [E]—du21   98-35818

Copyright © 1998 by Lemniscaat b.v. Rotterdam
Originally published in the Netherlands under the title Zonnebrand
by Lemniscaat b.v. Rotterdam
Printed and bound in Belgium

First American edition

Jung-Hee Spetter

# Lily and Trooper's Summer

Front Street 8 Lemniscaat

Asheville, North Carolina

"Hooray! No school today!"

"What are we going to do?"

"We're off to the beach."

"Mmmmm! The sun feels sooo good."

"Yikes! The water is cold."

Gurgle gurgle!

Pttooey!

"Look at my new dress. I love your swimcap."

"I've always wanted a fish."

"He's a real beauty."

"Come on, Trooper. Let's pick some flowers for him."

"Pick only the most beautiful ones."

"Yummy smell!"

"Oh, no! The bees are after us. Run!"

"Shoo! Go away, bees."

"Finally we're safe. We need a drink now."

"Let's play ball."

"Look what Trooper can do!"

"Let's pretend we're in the circus."

"Whoops!"

"Aren't we amazing? The Flying Girl and Her Amazing Dog, Trooper!"

"Thank you, Trooper. That feels nice."

"Good night, fish."

"No covers tonight. It's too hot."